Blue Moon Mountain

"for Zizi"
G.M.

Published in 2006 by Simply Read Books
www.simplyreadbooks.com

Cataloguing in Publication Data

McCaughrean, Geraldine
Blue moon mountain / Geraldine McCaughrean ; illustrated by Nicki Palin
and Tomislav Tomic.

For ages 5-9.

ISBN 10: 1-894965-56-6
ISBN 13: 978-1-894965-56-9

I. Palin, Nicki   II. Tomic, Tomislav   III. Title.

PZ7.M4784133Bl 2006   j823'.914
C2005-907305-5

First published in the UK by Templar Publishing

Designed by Mike Jolley & Nghiem Ta
Edited by Wendy Madgwick & Sue Harris

10 9 8 7 6 5 4 3 2 1

Printed in China

Blue Moon Mountain

Geraldine McCaughrean

Illustrated by Nicki Palin

and Tomislav Tomic

Simply Read Books

Once in a blue moon, as they say, the owl roars and the lion hoots and the magpie sings in key. The moonlight curds where it touches the ground—soft and sticky, then hard and bright, crazing beneath the softest step. And this white path leads across yard and garden, town and down, shore and moor to Blue Moon Mountain. There, do you see? Where the crags look like castles, and the clouds like flapping flags?

Only sleepers who sleep with their face to the window have ever seen such sights or such nights. And only the very brave (or the very foolish) have dared to follow that white, bright path. But Joy was born on a blue-moon night. She chose clothes the color of fire, and liked weather white with ice. And she dreamed dreams that were full of unicorns, and was forever asking her parents for stories and pictures of them.

Joy was born on a blue-moon night.

So when Joy woke on a blue-moon night, with a splash of moon in her face, her eyes were no sooner open than her feet were on the floor. For a step or two, the moonlight oozed and stuck and lifted on the soles of her feet. Then, as she started to run, it crackled like eggshells.

"Where are you going?" roared the owl.

"Where are you running?" hooted the lion.

"To find the Unicorn!" she cried.

The path led her through the yard. The flowers had no color and even the pond's fish were not gold in the blue-moonlight. The path led her through the town, but no one saw her go. The downs were grassy and the shore was sandy, and the moor was sharp with rocks. But the blue-moon path was as smooth as a tambourine, and her feet went drum-drum-drum as she ran.

Overhead the moon grew bigger and bigger from
winding together the white winds of the world; all the
winds and all the whispers, like a white ball of wool.

And when Joy finally stood and looked around her
on Blue Moon Mountain, the moonlight glimmered in
a hundred eyes watching, watching.

"Who's there? Who are you? I can see you!
Come out!" she called.

A winged piece of the mountain as big as a hill gaped
its jaws:

> "Where do they all live,
> The ones who don't exist?
> After the stories are over,
> Where do they never end?
> That is my riddle. Solve it who can."

A paw touched Joy on the shoulder. "That's the Sphinx," said a wolf who had appeared by her side. "Don't mind her. She never smiles."

"Oh I'm sorry," said Joy. "Why? Is she sad?"

"As sad as the rest of us," answered the Wolf. "It is rather sad, we find, Not to Exist."

"But you must exist," said Joy, "because I can see you!"

"Ah, well…" said the Wolf darkly. Then he broke off. "Forgive me saying so, but you don't seem very afraid."

"I'm sorry, should I be? I hope you're not offended."

"Not at all!" said the Wolf. "But I think it only my duty to warn you who I am. Do you know the story of Little Red Riding Hood? Or the Three Pigs? Well, I'm the Big Bad Wolf."

Joy looked at the Wolf with her head on one side. "I see," she said. "But you're not very big. And you seem rather friendly."

"Oh thank you," said the Wolf, "But you know what stories are. Someone has to be Bad. The giant. The troll. The wolf."

"But you must exist," said

Either the moon was growing brighter or her eyes were getting used to the dark. For all of a sudden Joy could make out other creatures walking on the mountain. There was a lion with wings and another with the body of a horse. There was a man made of snow, and another with the body of a horse. There were giant lizards, and dragons coiled around the roots of trees.

"I expect you'll run away now," said the Wolf sadly.

But Joy said, "Certainly not!" For surely here, on this strange mountain she would find her Unicorn.

The Big Bad Wolf seemed pleased. One by one he introduced her to the beasts of Blue Moon Mountain.

"This is the Hydra that Hercules fought. And this is the snake-headed Gorgon. You remember how, in the story, Perseus had to kill one without looking at it?"

But Joy was too young to know the stories. "I'm sorry, I thought you were a tree," she said turning to the Hydra. "And how lovely not to have to brush your hair in the morning," she said to the Gorgon.

Joy, "because I can see you!"

"**A**nd this is the Cockatrice who travelers said could strike a man dead just by one glance of its…"

"What nice eyes," said Joy, who was too young to know the story of the Cockatrice. "And does the Unicorn live here, too?"

"Yes, yes. It's here somewhere… But first let me introduce the Gulon of Sweden. Magicians hunt him for his teeth and paws… And here, the fire-breathing Dragon."

"I'm very pleased to meet you," said Joy. "I suppose you can cook your own dinner before you eat it!"

"And this is the Giant from the top of the Beanstalk. (That boy Jack was *such* a liar.) And this is the Troll who lived under the Billy Goats' bridge."

"Don't catch cold in those wet clothes," said Joy.

At the far side of Blue Moon Mountain lay a great lake. Mermaids and silkies lolled on the shore, flicking their fishy tails in the surf. The sea monster Orc splashed about in the shallows, showering them with spray. The Big Bad Wolf carried Joy down to the waterside to meet them on his soft brown back.

"This Mountain is very crowded," she said.

"There is nowhere else we can go," sighed the Wolf. "When all those stories and legends are finished, we've served our purpose, haven't we? We've proved how brave the hero in the story is to have fought us, or killed us, or escaped our fearful paws? Of course the storytellers never say anything good about us. '*How fierce it was,*' they say. '*How hideous! How dangerous! How huge! How wicked,*' And we're not really like that at all. They only say it to prove that *they* are good and brave."

"It's not easy, you know, when no one wants to know you. We daren't leave the Mountain, you see. People out there would be too afraid. Because of all those stories. Mostly they choose to say we don't exist at all—except in their imaginations."

"Oh, but that's such a shame. After all, you're so *beautiful*!" cried Joy. The Wolf blushed. "But you are! You're marvelous! Look how golden the Wyvern's scales are. Look how the Cockatrice dances! How the Salamander glows in the dark! Look at the dear little Catoblepas! I've always dreamed of seeing a Unicorn, of course, but I never knew there were so many other creatures just as fine!"

A murmur ran up and down the Mountain: "She says we are fine."

"… says we're marvelous."

"… says we're all as lovely as the Unicorn."

"And she's not frightened of us at all!"

"What, not even of the Kraken?"

"*Ah! The Kraken.*"

"Which of you is the Kraken?" asked Joy.

"He's Out There," said the others, pointing over the deep, deep, dark-blue lake.

"He's rising now. Listen, you can hear him. The lake is over a thousand fathoms deep, and he rises from the bottom to the top."

"Only once in a blue moon," added the Wolf.

The Wyvern trembled. The Salamander shivered. The mermaids clung to the silkies and the Cyclops shut his one eye. Even the beasts of Blue Moon Mountain were plainly afraid.

Such a long, long time it took for the Kraken to rise—the world's greatest monster from the world's deepest lair. But at last one black tentacle waved above the water. One, then two, then a forest of tentacles, each one with a thousand suckers, slippery with purple slime. Huge waves spread from the spot, broke on the shore, and spray drenched them all. Many a monster shut its eyes.

"Oh, what a wonderful creature!" cried Joy, and stood on tiptoe to wave back.

"She says the Kraken's wonderful," murmured the Gryphon in surprise.

"Well, it is rather grand, I suppose," the Gulon thought aloud as he looked at the creature from the deep.

One by one the beasts waved back at the Kraken's waving tentacles, and it grew so excited that it stirred up breakers so huge that they almost touched the moon.

"Oh, what a wonderful creature!"

"The Moon!" cried the creatures, looking up at the lightening sky. "The moon is setting!"

"Quick! You must leave the Mountain before the white path breaks!" said the Wolf.

But it was too late.

As Joy ran back to the path, its eggshell whiteness changed beneath her feet to a sticky softness. It began to melt away. "Oh! How shall I get home now?" she cried.

"Not until the next blue moon," said the Sphinx darkly, "and who can tell when that might be?"

"Oh! How shall I ge

"Don't worry. One of the Winged Ones will fly you home," said the Wolf smartly. "Pegasus, the winged horse…"

"Who me?" said the horse. "Leave the Mountain after the moon has set? I cannot! I am too afraid!"

"The giant Roc, then," suggested the Wolf. "It's no distance for a bird half as big as the sky,"

"Who me?" said the Roc. "Leave the Mountain after the white path's dissolved? How would I find my way back?"

"The Gryphon, then, or the Harpy or the Simurgh or a raft of fairies…"

But none of the winged Ones dared to make the journey so close to the set of the moon.

…ome now?" she cried.

"**I shall take her!**" It was the Phoenix. "I'm near my end, so I'll soon begin again," it said puzzlingly. "Won't you ride astride my back, girl-child?"

The creatures all cheered. And yet even Joy was a *little* afraid. The elderly Phoenix was starting to turn very red, and to smoke at the wingtips. He was quite hot to the touch. She slipped between his great wings and clung tight round his neck, and the Phoenix soared into the sky just as the moon began to sink behind the Mountain.

"I know the answer to your riddle," Joy called to the Sphinx. "On Blue Moon Mountain! *That's* where you live,

>The Ones who don't exist
>And after the stories are over,
>This is where they never end!"

"Is that what you think?" called the Sphinx who always answers everything with a question.

"On Blue Moon Mountain! That's where..."

The Phoenix began to glow a little with heat. "I never die," it explained. "I just lay my egg, burst into flames, and the heat of the fire hatches the egg: and there I am—made new again!"

"Oh good," said Joy, hoping the Phoenix would not burst into flames just yet. The white path melted beneath them as if rain had washed it away. They flew over moor and shore, down and town, the dark park and the lit street, the garden and the houses, and all the while the Phoenix grew hotter and the moon sank lower in the sky.

"Home again," said the Phoenix.

"Only just in time," hooted the lion.

"Did you see the Unicorn?" roared the owl.

"Well, would you believe it!" exclaimed Joy. "In the end I quite forgot to look for him."

They flew over moor and shore...

Back on the mountain the Unicorn darted out of hiding. "Where is she? Gone?" he asked.

"She had to go. The moon was setting," said the Wolf. "Why did you not show yourself before?"

"I was saving the best till last," said the vain creature. "It was *me* she came to see! Not you! She came to see me! I heard her say so! Why else would she come? I'm the most beautiful creature in all the world—and what are *you*?"

"We're *wonderful*," said the other beasts and birds, swaggering up and down. "*She* said so. We're *beautiful*!" And suddenly it seemed as if all their sadness had melted along with the white moon-path.

"**I**f she thought you were wonderful, what would she think of me?" bragged the Unicorn. And he sprang off the Mountain and into the air, shouting, "Look at me, girl-child! Look at me! Look at me!" It was a jump so huge that it crossed moor and shore, down and town, yard and garden and the Unicorn landed on the sill of Joy's bedroom window—just as the moon set.

"I am the Unicorn, creature of myths and wishes, famed in story and history… Er, can I come in?" he said.

"Certainly," said Joy opening the window. "It's lovely to see you. But weren't you rather silly to leave the Mountain? How will you get back?"

"Oh! I don't know," said the Unicorn, who was famously foolish.

"You'll have to wait, I suppose, until the next blue moon," said Joy, shaking her head.

"Certainly," said Joy… "It's lovely to see you."

And it was many years before

The Unicorn hung its head. "But if people see me, they'll chase me and try to catch me and lock me in a cage."

"Then I shall have to hide you here," said Joy. "But you must be very quiet and only come out when I say so."

So after that Joy did not ask her father, "Draw me a Unicorn," for she could look at one whenever she pleased.

And she never asked her mother, "Tell me a story about Unicorns," for she and her friend shared adventures enough in the secret dark.

But often when she heard a story about the Big Bad Wolf, or the Troll, or the Gorgon, or of fire-breathing dragons, she would interrupt and say, "Are you sure that's how they were?" She drew some quite marvelous pictures, too (though some people said they were frightening) of birds and beasts and monsters.

And it was many years before Joy and the Unicorn went back to Blue Moon Mountain. For it is only once in a blue moon that the owl roars and the lion hoots and the moon lays down a path to show the way…

oy and the Unicorn went back…

The Creatures

CATOBLEPAS

This strange creature, which resembled a small, winged buffalo, is said to have lived on the African high plains and desert land near the sources of the Nile. It fed only on poisonous plants. It had a curly tail, a heavy mane of stiff, bristly hair and was covered with scales. The Catoblepas's great head was so heavy it could barely lift it. Ancient tales of this curious beast tell how one glance from its strange eyes would strike a creature dead.

COCKATRICE

The Cockatrice, or Basilisk, had the head and body of a cock, leathery, spiked wings, and a long, barbed serpent's tail. Ancient myths tell how the Cockatrice's poisonous breath could scorch plants and split rocks asunder. One glance from its scarlet eyes was enough to kill, and even the evil hissing sound it made could cause death. Only three things could kill it: a weasel, a cock crowing, or the sight of its own image.

CYCLOPES

Cyclopes, a mythical race of giants, looked like hairy human beings except that they had only one eye in the center of their forehead. Wild, savage creatures, they kept herds of giant goats and sheep and lived in caves. Odysseus and his men were captured and imprisoned in a cave by the cyclops Polyphemus. Odysseus and his crew blinded the giant, and escaped by clinging beneath the sheep as they left the cave.

DRAGONS

Legends from all over the world depict dragons as giant fire-breathing, winged reptiles. Their name comes from the Greek word for serpent, but dragons from different regions vary greatly. Many had magical powers. In Norse myths, dragons were a symbol of war and guarded the burial mounds of warriors. Chinese dragons were the companions of the weather gods. In Europe dragons were regarded as evil creatures.

GORGONS

The gorgons were three sisters who lived on a remote island in ancient Greece. They had the bodies of women, with hideous faces, the teeth of hogs and their fingernails were brass claws. But the most spectacular feature was their hair—a mass of live, hissing snakes. Any human who dared to look at them was instantly turned to stone. Two of the gorgons were immortal, but legend says that the third, Medusa, was killed by Perseus.

GRYPHON

The Gryphon, or Griffin, was a fierce beast with a lion's body, legs and tail and the wings and head of an eagle, but with pointed dog's ears. It is said that Gryphons were native to India. They lived in wild mountainous countryside, building their nests, which were said to be lined with gold, on high cliff-tops. Gryphons also served the gods as guardians, and were often used as symbols of wisdom and heroism.

The Creatures

GULON

The savage Gulon lived in the wilds of Sweden. About the size of a large dog, this fearsome creature had the face and ears of a cat with long sharp teeth and claws. Its thick furry coat was soft and beautifully patterned and its tail was bushy like that of a fox. It fed only on the carcasses of dead animals and would eat and eat until its body swelled up like a balloon. It was hunted for its skin, and its teeth were used in magical spells.

HARPY

The Harpy was a fearsome creature that lived in ancient Greece. It had the body and wings of a giant bird and the head of an ugly old woman. Harpies were always hungry. Most of their food was snatched from humans. Foul-smelling, these creatures covered everything they touched with filth so that it was useless. Their monstrous appetites were never satisfied and the unfortunate people that they visited regularly would eventually starve.

HYDRA

The Hydra, a huge snake-like monster with several hideous heads, lived in ancient Greece. One whiff of its poisonous breath caused death. It seemed impossible to kill. When one of its fearsome heads was cut off, two grew in its place. The Hydra was destroyed by the hero Heracles. Each time he cut off a head, Heracles sealed the stump with a flame to stop new ones growing. The last immortal head he buried under a stone.

KRAKEN

Long ago, Norse sailors told tales of an enormous sea creature with a huge body, eight long tentacles and fiery red eyes—the Kraken. It lived deep within the sea, occasionally rising to the surface to attack unwary sailors. The monster would entwine the ship within its tentacles then slowly sink beneath the waves, dragging the boat and crew to the depths in a powerful whirlpool. People now believe this creature to be the giant squid.

MERMAIDS

Stories of mermaids have been told throughout the world for thousands of years. These creatures, which lived in the seas, had the body of a beautiful woman from the waist up, and the lower body of a fish. Sailors told tales of mermaids sitting on rocks, combing their hair and singing, to lure the men away from their ships so they would drown. They had powers over the sea and if angry could make giant waves that sank ships and flooded villages.

ORC

The Orc was a medieval sea monster that was greatly feared by sailors. They told many tales of how this fearsome beast would pursue and devour any creatures that came within its reach. It would even pursue its prey into the shallows, snapping at it with its huge teeth. Today, people believe that the creature they described was probably the killer whale, or Orca, which is indeed a skilled hunter of fish and seals.

The Creatures

PEGASUS

The winged horse Pegasus was the offspring of the Greek God Poseidon and Medusa. Although he had sprung from the ugly monster's severed head, Pegasus was a splendid creature. Bellerophon, a Greek hero, captured Pegasus with a magical golden bridal. Together they flew to the cave of the two-headed monster Chimera. With the help of Pegasus, the youth completed the task he had been set and killed the creature.

PHOENIX

The rarest and most beautiful of all mythical birds was the Phoenix. There was only one Phoenix, which lived for at least 500 years. When its end approached, the bird would build a nest of sweet-smelling wood and herbs. At dawn, it would set fire to the nest and would be consumed by the flames. But as the flames died down, the Phoenix would rise again from its own ashes, young and strong, a symbol of immortality.

ROC

A gigantic legendary bird, the Roc, or Rukh, was said to be so huge that when in flight, it would blot out the sun, casting a huge shadow over the land below. Legend says that the females fed their young on elephants. Marco Polo described the bird in his travels through Madagascar and Africa, and *The Tales of the Arabian Nights* tell how Sinbad the Sailor, cast ashore on a desert island, came upon a giant Roc egg.

SPHINX

In Greek myths, a Sphinx was a monster with a woman's head and the body of a lion. Some Sphinx asked travelers riddles and if they could not answer, ate them. The city of Thebes was terrorized by a Sphinx, who asked travelers, "What animal goes on four feet in the morning, on two at noon, and three feet in the evening?" The hero Oedipus gave the right answer—man. The Sphinx was so angry she killed herself.

UNICORN

The Unicorn exists in the legends and heraldry of many countries. A beautiful white horse-like creature with a long, spiral horn in the centre of its forehead, it lived in meadows and forests. The Unicorn's horn, or alicorn, was reputed to have special powers. It was said that it could protect against poisons, fits and fevers. A symbol of purity, this mysterious beast could only be captured by a young unmarried maiden.

WYVERN

A mythical flying serpent, the Wyvern looked very like a two-legged dragon with enormous wings. Its tail was often barbed and its claws were said to be like an eagle's talons. As with the dragon, there are many tales of the fire-breathing Wyvern terrorizing villages and carrying off people to its lair. Both winged and wingless Wyverns are important symbols in heraldry, and have often been used in royal ensigns.